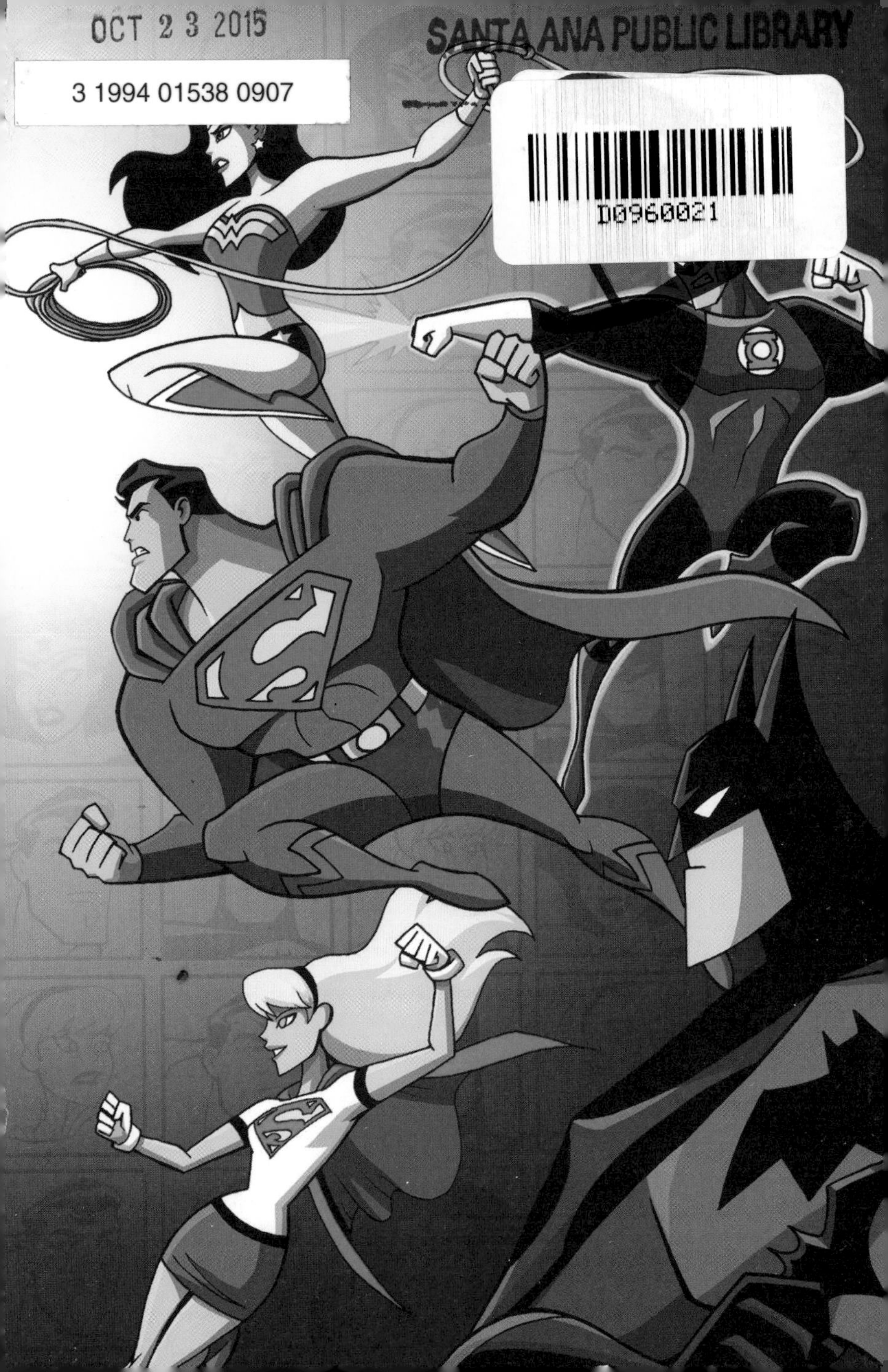

SUPERMAN VS. BIZARRO

WRITTEN BY
JOHN SAZAKLIS

ILLUSTRATED BY
LUCIANO VECCHIO

SUPERMAN CREATED BY
JERRY SIEGEL AND JOE SHUSTER
BY SPECIAL ARRANGEMENT WITH
THE JERRY SIEGEL FAMILY

STONE ARCH BOOKS
a capstone imprint

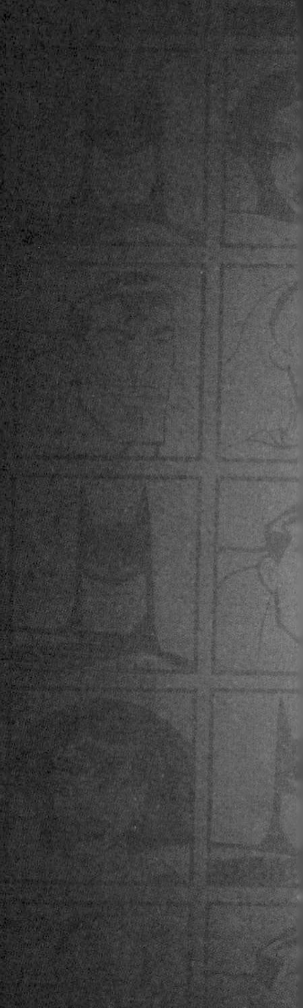

Published by Stone Arch Books in 2013
A Capstone Imprint
1710 Roe Crest Drive
North Mankato, MN 56003
www.capstonepub.com

STAR29363

Cataloging-in-Publication Data is available at the Library of Congress website
ISBN: 978-1-4342-6012-3 (library binding)

Summary: Bizarro is back! This backward version of Superman has plans to remake the Earth in his own image, and he's not taking No--or, is that Yes?--for an answer. Can the Man of Steel save the day before this evil opposite turns Earth into an alternate reality?

Designed by Hilary Wacholz

Printed in China by Nordica.
1114/CA21401695
102014 008591R

TABLE OF CONTENTS

SUPERMAN™

REAL NAME: Kal-El (Clark Kent)

ROLE: Super hero

BASE: Metropolis

ABILITIES: Superman hails from the planet Krypton, but he grew up on planet Earth as Clark Kent. Fueled by the solar radiation of Earth's yellow sun, Superman's superpowers include: invulnerability, flight, heat vision, X-ray vision, super-strength, and super-speed. Like all Kryptonians, Superman is vulnerable to Kryptonite.

BIZARRO

REAL NAME: Unknown

ROLE: Super-villain

BASE: Mobile

ABILITIES: Bizarro Superman is a botched clone of Superman. This doppelganger's superpowers are the exact opposite of Superman's. While he tries to be just like the Man of Steel, he never quite gets it right and ends up causing trouble, instead.

CHAPTER 1

BIZARRO SUPERMAN

In the top-secret S.T.A.R. Labs, Dr. Hamilton was hard at work on his latest experiment. He had been up for many hours straight, and was bleary-eyed from staring at his computer screen. Morning was approaching and the sun would rise in minutes, but he refused to go home and sleep until his research was complete.

"Maybe a cup of coffee will help me stay up a few more hours," he said to himself.

KLANG! As he put on his coat, Dr. Hamilton heard a loud sound coming from the main lab.

"No one should be in the building at this hour," the worried scientist said to himself. He picked up a heavy monkey wrench and left his office.

Dr. Hamilton walked stealthily down the hall. The clanging got louder and louder as he moved closer to the cryogenics lab. **CLANG! CLANG! CLANG!**

Reaching the laboratory's entrance, Dr. Hamilton swallowed hard and peeked into the lab through the tiny window inside the door. **FZZT! FZZT!** Sparks sizzled and smoke hissed out of a sleeping chamber.

Raising the wrench, the doctor opened the door and charged into the room.

"Don't move!" cried Dr. Hamilton. Suddenly, a wide, flat panel atop the sleeping chamber slowly slid open.

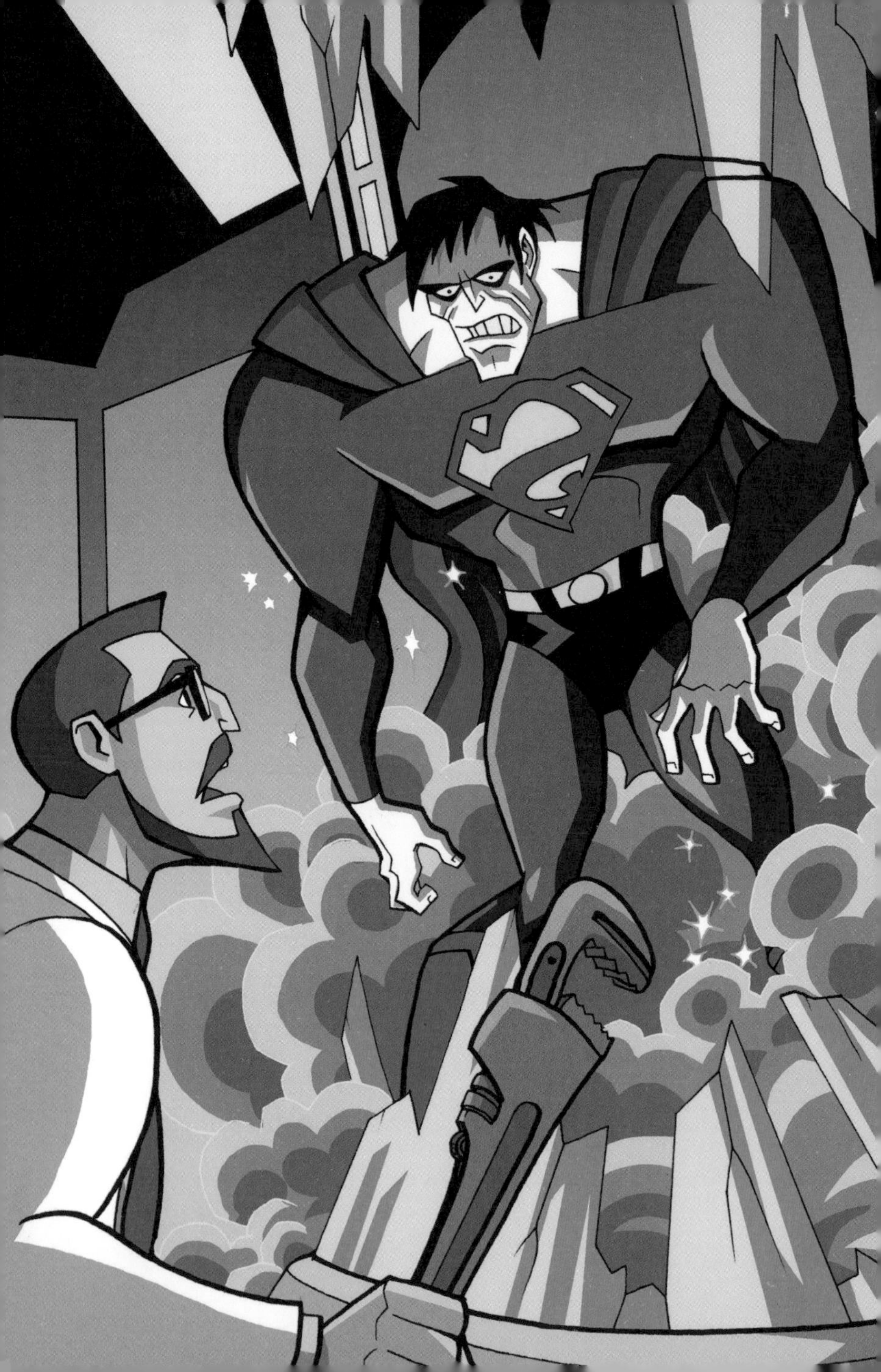

Dr. Hamilton stared in horror. A creature named Bizarro yawned and stretched his arms overhead. His eyes opened. He sat upright. Then he turned and locked eyes with Dr. Hamilton.

"Hurrgh?!" growled the disoriented doppelganger. He gripped the side of the apparatus. **CRUNCH!** The metal edge crumpled in his hand as if it were paper. Bizarro continued mumbling unintelligibly as he pulled himself out of the sleeping chamber.

Bizarro's face twitched as the clone's memories of the secret lab and the scary scientists came rushing back. "Bizarro no want doctors!" he yelled.

CRASH! Bizarro smashed through the ceiling.

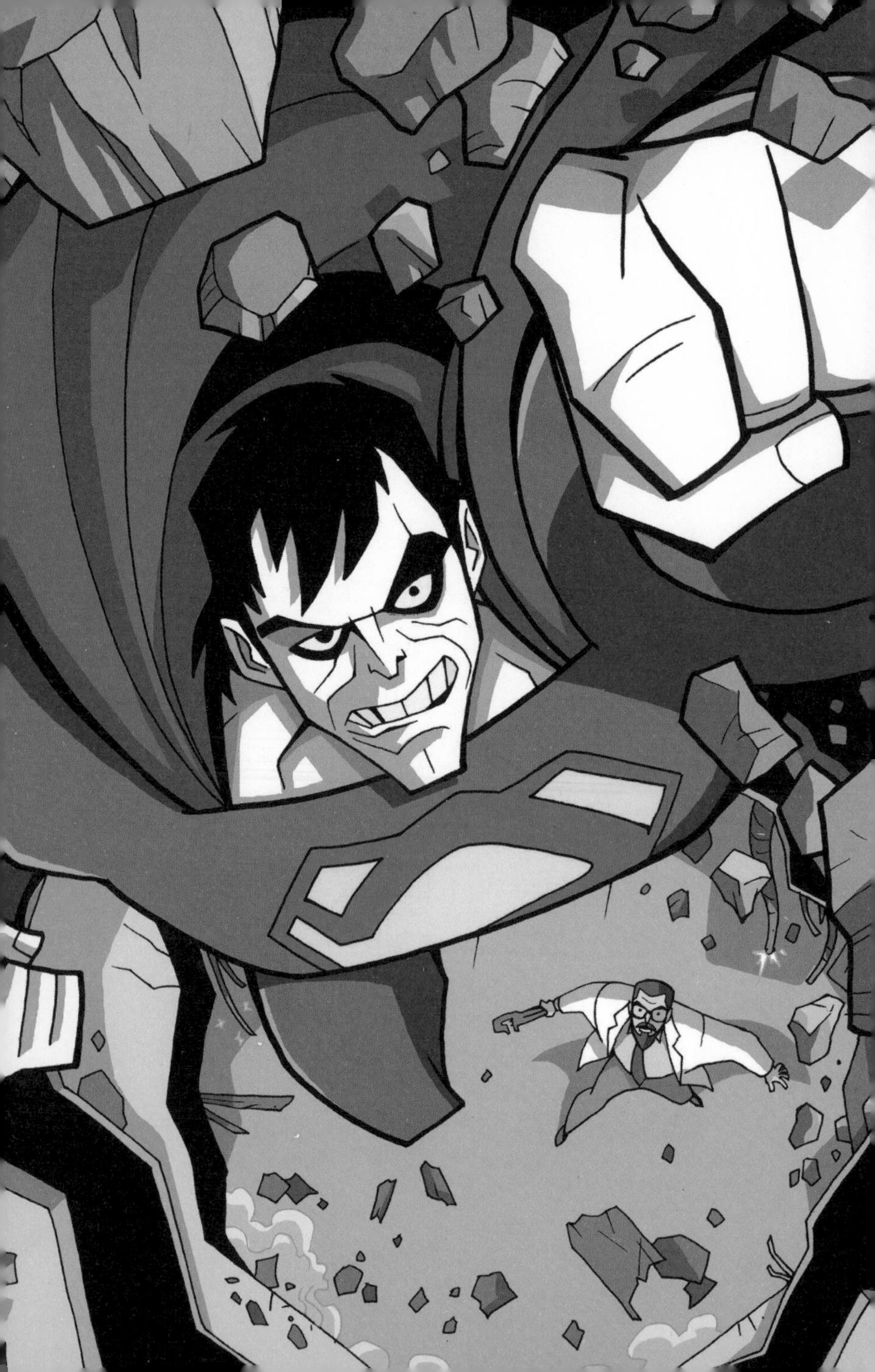

CHAPTER 2

THE MAN OF STEEL

Dr. Hamilton watched Bizarro bolt through the laboratory's new skylight "I think I need to contact Superman," he said.

The next morning, sixth-grader Marc and his older sister, Anna, were on a school bus headed for Metropolis. All of the middle school art classes were taking a class trip to the Museum of Art.

Marc reached into his backpack and took out his digital camera. He liked to take pictures everywhere he went, documenting everything in sight.

Anna, on the other hand, kept a journal. She wrote stories about all the different things she did with her brother.

They were sure that visiting Metropolis would be exciting, but so far, their trip had been pretty uneventful.

Marc pressed his face against the window. "Look, it's the Daily Planet Building!" he said. He snapped pictures with his digital camera.

Anna noticed the big, brass globe atop the roof of the Daily Planet Building as the bus turned onto a high bridge.

"I would love to work there someday," Anna said. "I want to be a respected journalist like Lois Lane!"

"And I want to take pictures just like the *Daily Planet* photographer Jimmy Olsen!" Marc said.

Suddenly, a front tire burst. **POP!**

The bus careened into oncoming traffic.

Cars swerved out of the way to avoid a collision. **SKREEEEECH!**

The bus driver frantically turned the wheel, but the vehicle was already out of control. It crashed through the divider. **CRUNCH!** The bus jutted out over the edge of the bridge, dangling precariously.

The terrified teachers tried to comfort the screaming middle-schoolers. As the bus swayed back and forth, the metal frame slid closer and closer to the edge.

"Everyone, get to the back of the bus!" ordered the driver. "Shifting weight will keep the bus from falling!"

While everyone else panicked, Marc continued to use his camera. **CLICK!**

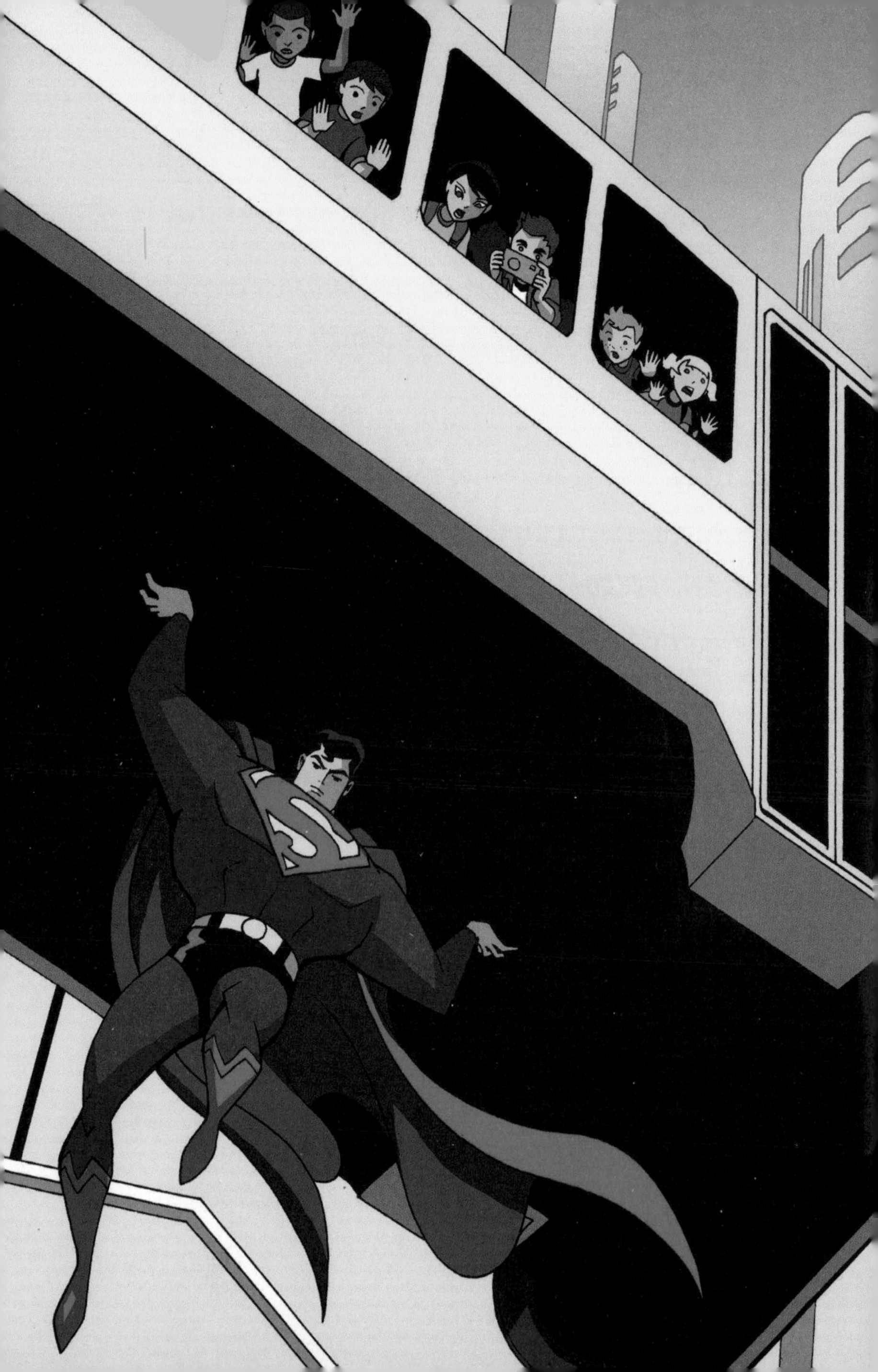

"This isn't the time for pictures!" Anna yelled.

"Yes it is," Marc said as he pointed out the window as a red and blue blur streaked across the sky.

"Is that a comet?" asked a nearby student.

"No, it's Superman!" Anna squealed.

Instantly, the front end of the bus lifted upward. It was no longer facing down at the river, but up at the bright blue sky. Everyone on the bus gripped their seats.

A few moments later, there was a slight rumble and a **THUD!** The bus stopped moving. It was now resting on a side street in midtown Metropolis.

Clearly shaken, the passengers and driver slowly filed out from the bus.

In front of them was the Museum of Art, lined with Greek columns and statues.

"Welcome to Metropolis," said a deep voice from behind the visitors. They turned to see the Man of Steel standing before them. He had a big smile on his face. "I hope this unfortunate accident doesn't change your opinion of our fair city."

Everyone was speechless. The group could not believe they were standing in front of the Man of Steel himself!

Superman graciously shook their hands while using his X-ray vision to make sure no one was injured. Anna continued to stare in wide-eyed amazement. Marc slowly took a single photo of Superman shaking his sister's hand. **CLICK!**

"Marc!" Anna said. "You didn't even ask him permission."

Superman chuckled. "It's okay," he said to Anna and Marc. "I'm used to it."

With his heat vision, Superman zapped the torn rubber of the tire. **ZRRRRRRRT!** When it was soft and malleable enough, he cooled it with his freeze breath. Once the hole was sealed, Superman filled the tire up by blowing into it with his super-breath.

"There you go, sir," Superman said to the bus driver. "That should get you to the nearest service station. Enjoy the rest of your day!"

The bus driver smiled and said, "Thanks so much!"

And with that, Superman waved goodbye and flew up and away into the air.

Across the street, two *Daily Planet* reporters climbed out of a taxi. A woman looked over her shoulder at a redheaded photographer trying to keep up with her.

"Move it, Jimmy!" she said. "We want to report the news before it becomes history!"

"It's Lois Lane and Jimmy Olsen," Marc whispered in awe to Anna. "This day just keeps getting better!"

The two siblings eagerly hurried toward the front of the class. As Lois and Jimmy introduced themselves, Anna interrupted them. "We know who you are," she said.

"We're your biggest fans!" Marc added.

Lois and Jimmy grinned and shook their hands. "The Museum of Art will be pretty dull after being rescued by Superman," Anna said, beaming with excitement.

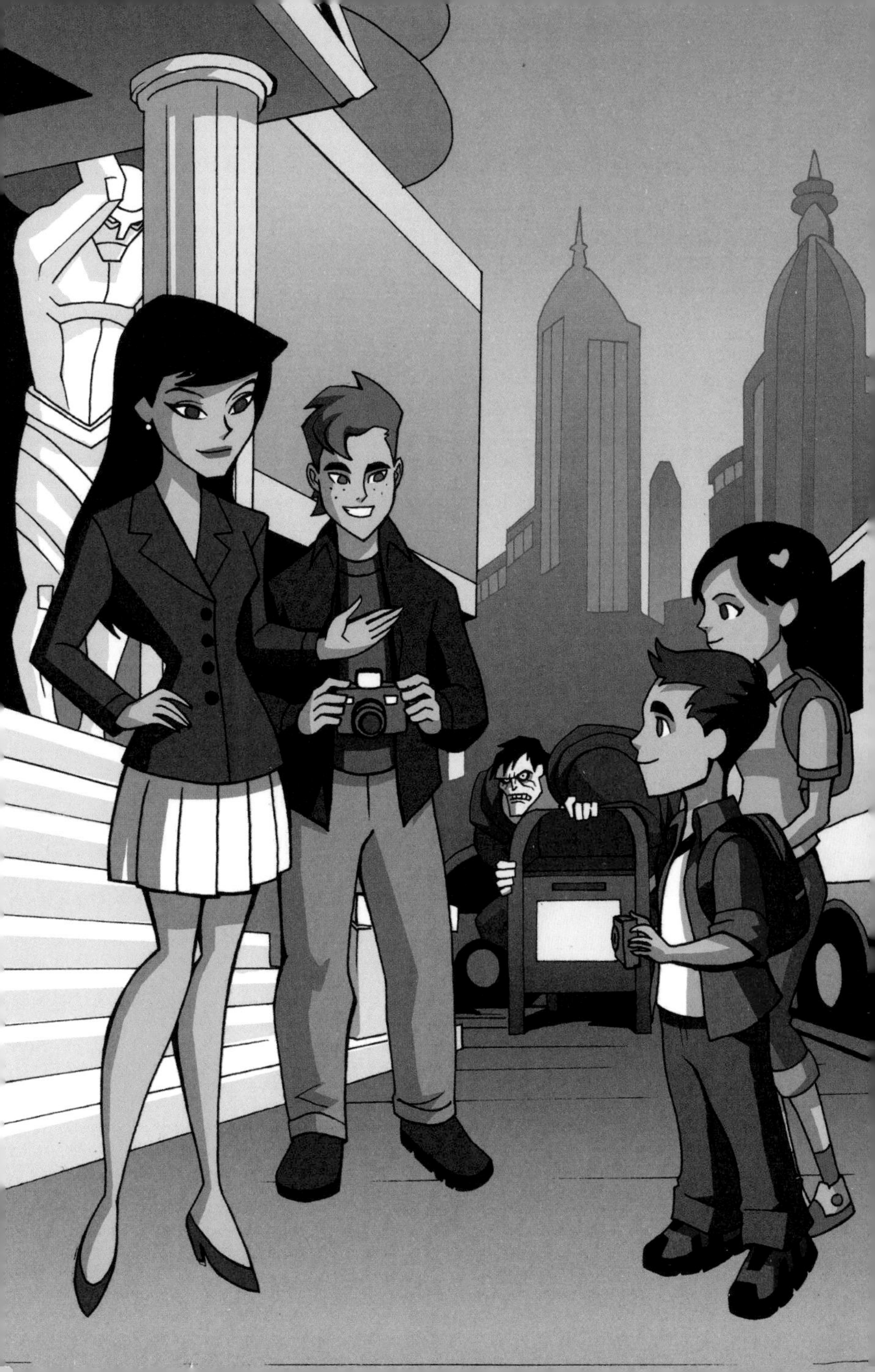

"Believe me, I know!" Lois said, smiling.

The group was too distracted to notice that they were being watched. The man tried to hide behind a short, metal mailbox. But his large figure wasn't even half-concealed.

It was Bizarro. Now back in Metropolis, the backward double had seen Superman save the day once again . . . and he was jealous.

"Bizarro am hero, too!" he said to himself. **CRUNCH!** The side of the mailbox collapsed between his fingers. "Me have idea!" Bizarro flew toward the museum, ready to put his plan into action.

CHAPTER 3

BIZARRO'S BIG ADVENTURE

Shortly after the reporters left the museum, the teachers finally calmed the children down. Then they headed into the museum for their class tour. Marc and Anna hid behind one of the tall pillars on the steps, watching everyone else pass by.

"Can you believe that just happened?" Anna whispered. "This is going to make a fantastic entry in the school newspaper. I need to write about it right now!"

"And I have the pictures to prove it," Marc answered, holding up his camera.

The siblings were distracted by a shadow hovering overhead. Marc and Anna looked up into the sky. As the shape came into focus, the children could see that it was a muscular man in tights with a bright cape billowing in the wind behind him.

"Superman is back!" Anna exclaimed.

When the flying man landed on the steps in front of the youngsters, it was clear this man was not Superman.

"Me not Superman," the figure said reluctantly. "Me am —"

"Bizarro," Anna finished, surprising the newcomer.

"You know Bizarro how?" Bizarro replied scratching his head. "Me know you not."

"We read about you in the newspaper," Anna said as calmly as she could.

"Lois Lane wrote a story about how you kidnapped her, then brought her to a secret lab. Then Superman came to the rescue."

"Bizarro not kidnap!" the duplicate declared. "Me try to save Lois. Me am hero like Superman, but nobody understand!"

"May I take your picture?" Marc asked.

Bizarro clapped his hands with glee. "YES!" he cried. "You are take many pictures of Bizarro!"

Then he pointed to Anna. "And you are write stories of Bizarro! Friends we is now. Metropolis see Bizarro am great hero!"

"Sounds good to me!" Marc exclaimed.

Anna frowned. She pulled Marc aside by the arm. "In her story, Lois wrote that Bizarro was a danger to himself and others," she whispered.

"Yes, but we can help him," Marc said. "He just needs a little guidance." Marc looked up at his sister and gave her the big puppy dog eyes. Now she couldn't say no.

Anna sighed. "Okay, we'll help Bizarro be a hero," she said. "But we have to get back here by 3 pm before our bus leaves."

"Yes, Bizarro bring you back when you done," Bizarro said. As he spoke, his voice became more and more excited. "But first you write pictures and take stories! Show Metropolis that Bizarro am helpful hero and me be your friend!"

Bizarro scooped up a sibling in each arm. "Bizarro's big adventure begins now!"

WOOOOOOSH! He bounded high into the air. The unlikely trio soared over the museum and headed toward a nearby park.

Marc and Anna looked down and saw a large tree-lined field with a stone statue of Superman in the center. Beyond the sculpture was a shimmering lake with tourists paddle-boating in the water.

Anna held her breath. She had never experienced Metropolis from this point of view. She was certain that few people had.

Bizarro used his super-vision to scan the area. He was looking for an opportunity to do something heroic. As luck would have it, he spotted something almost immediately.

"New friends, look down there!" Bizarro said. He pointed to a tall oak tree. Four people beneath it looked frightened.

"I think they need our help," Marc said.

"Bizarro is going to be big hero!" the clone cried and zoomed down to the park.

The flying friends landed in front of a mother, a father, and their two children. The little ones were wiping away tears.

Anna approached them and bent down on one knee. Marc got his camera ready.

"What's the matter?" Anna asked.

"Miss Kitty!" they sobbed in unison.

"Miss Kitty is our cat," the mother explained. "She climbed up this tree and now she's too scared to climb down."

"We're all out of ideas," the father said. "It's a good thing you arrived when you did, Superman!"

Bizarro stepped closer. Each member of the family stepped back.

"Me not Superman!" he shouted. "Me am Bizarro, me am great hero!"

Anna put her hand on Bizarro's arm to calm the doppelganger.

"Bizarro, that cat is stuck in the tree," she said. "We need to get her down and give her back to her family. Can you help?"

"Yes," Bizarro said, nodding his head.

He looked up and saw the poor tabby cat cowering on the edge of a thick branch. "Tree is hurting kitty," Bizarro said. "Must save kitty."

Before anyone could react, Bizarro pushed his fingers into the bark of the tree. **CRUNCH!** Tensing his legs and squatting slightly, Bizarro emitted a giant grunt and ripped the tree out of the ground!

The family gasped. Gnarled, mangled tree roots dangled in the air as clumps of dirt dropped all around them.

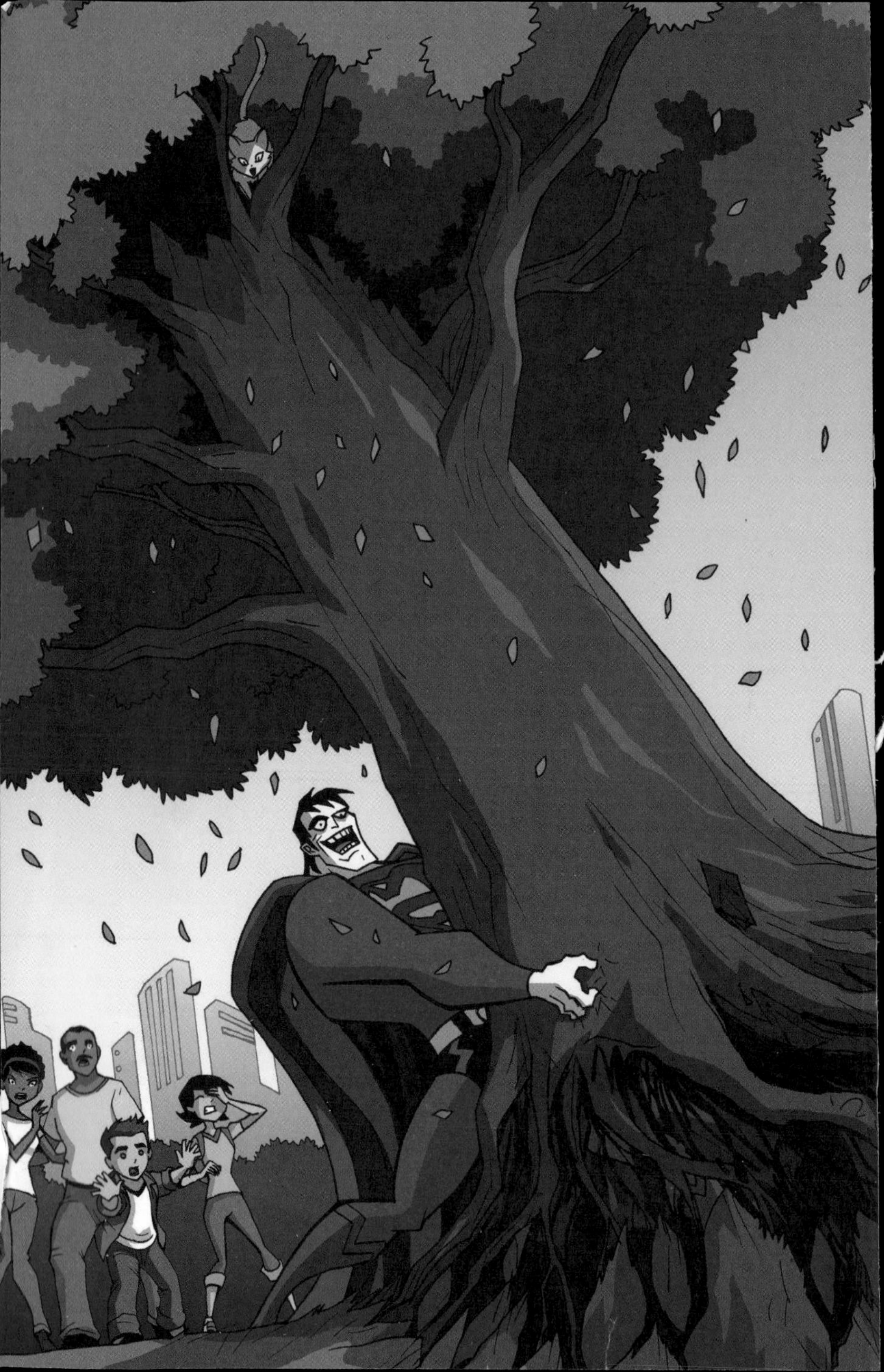

With another loud grunt, Bizarro turned
the tree on its side and shook it. SWISH!
SWISH! SWISH! Leaves scattered off
their branches, covering everyone nearby.
A few startled birds took to the air.

Now that the ground was much closer,
the frightened feline confidently jumped to
safety. The two children picked Miss Kitty
up and hugged her close. Bizarro righted
the tree and shoved it back into the gaping
hole in the ground.

"Bizarro save kitty," he boomed,
clapping the dirt off his hands. He clenched
his crooked teeth into a smile.

The family was grateful, but also a little
scared. They hurriedly thanked Bizarro and
scurried off as quickly as possible. Marc
had been snapping pictures the whole time.
When he finished, he ran over.

"That was . . . good, Bizarro," Marc said, giving the bumbling brute a high-five. "But it was pretty weird, too."

"You need to be more careful, Bizarro," Anna added. "You could have hurt us all when you pulled out that tree!"

"Before kitty stuck. Now kitty not stuck," Bizarro replied. "No is problem!"

"Yes, but be more careful," said Marc. "And please replant that tree."

Bizarro shrugged. He picked up the tree and slammed it back in place with a resounding **THUD!**

"Don't be afraid to ask us for help," Anna added. "We'll solve things together."

Suddenly, there was a loud thundering sound. **RUMMMBLE!** The ground shook beneath their feet.

Bizarro picked up Marc and Anna and soared high into the air.

Looking out over the park into the heart of the city, the three friends saw an amazing sight — a giant robot! The mechanical marvel stood almost thirty stories tall. Its metallic shell gleamed in the sunlight as it trudged toward the Daily Planet Building. RUMMMBLE! Every step it took felt like a small earthquake.

"That can't be good!" Anna shouted.

"Just another day in Metropolis!" Marc shouted back. He clutched his camera so he wouldn't lose it.

"Big robot are bad," Bizarro said. "Big bad robot is make Bizarro big hero!"

With the youngsters in tow, Bizarro zoomed toward the building — and straight into the path of the rampaging robot!

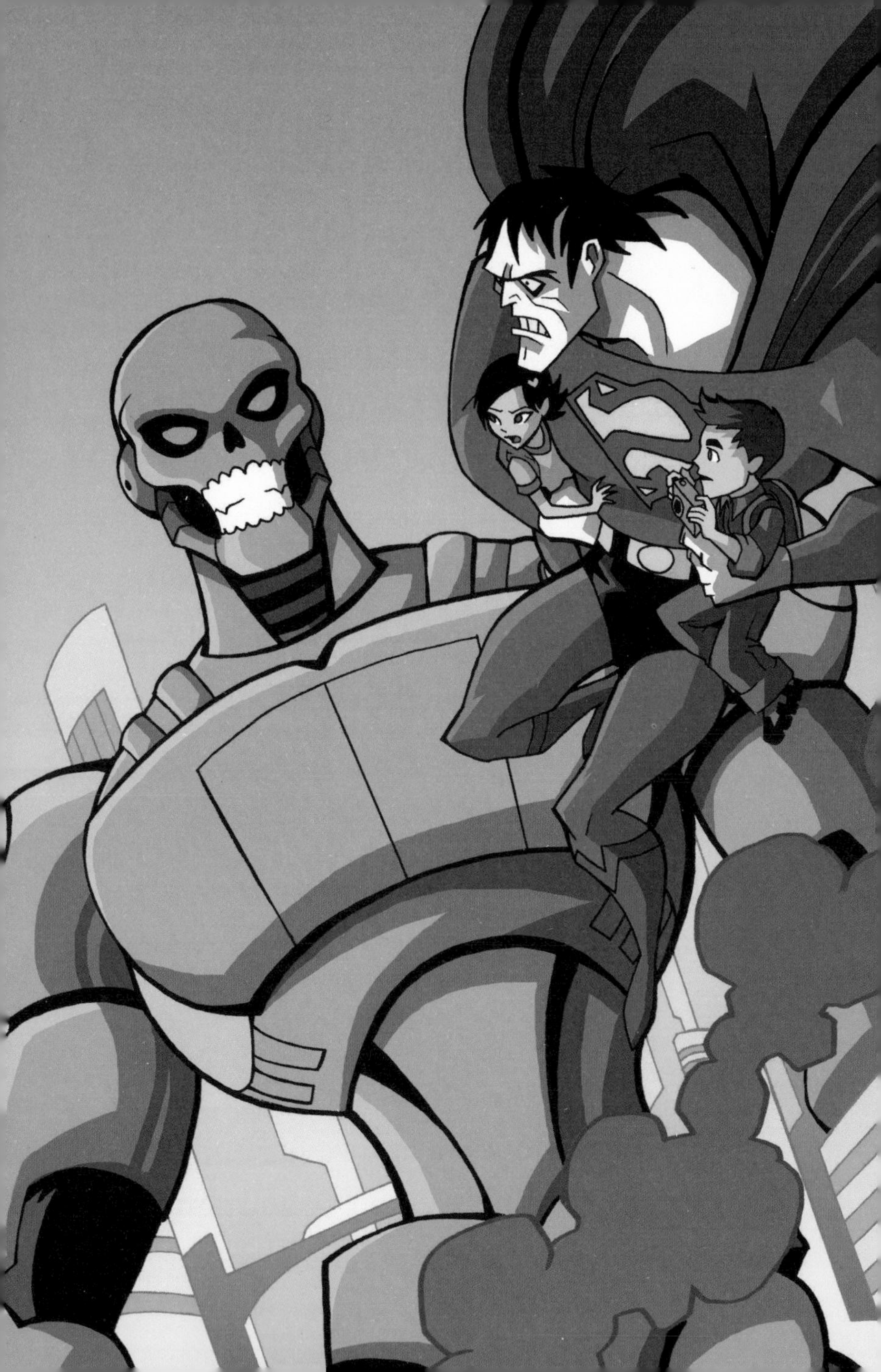

CHAPTER 4

TO THE... RESCUE?

"Where are you, Superman?!" shouted the metallic monster.

He pounded the ground with his massive foot. The tremors set off car alarms within a five-block radius.

"There's a new 'Man of Steel' in town! **HA HA HA!**" The hulking hunk of metal transformed one of his arms into a plasma cannon and aimed it directly at the globe atop the Daily Planet Building. "Prepare yourselves for the end of the world!"

Metallo's real name was John Corben. Long ago, his brain had been transplanted into an artificial cybernetic body. He had one goal: to destroy Superman.

ZAAAAP! The wicked machine man fired his powerful weapon. In an instant, Superman intercepted the energy blast by shielding the globe with his body. **ZRRRRT!** The laser beam fizzled into a shower of harmless sparks.

"You're not welcome here, Metallo!" Superman bellowed. "I stopped you once before, and I will stop you again."

"So you think, Superman!" Metallo replied. "I've made some improvements in my design since our last encounter . . ."

Metallo opened his chest plate to reveal a chunk of glowing green rock.

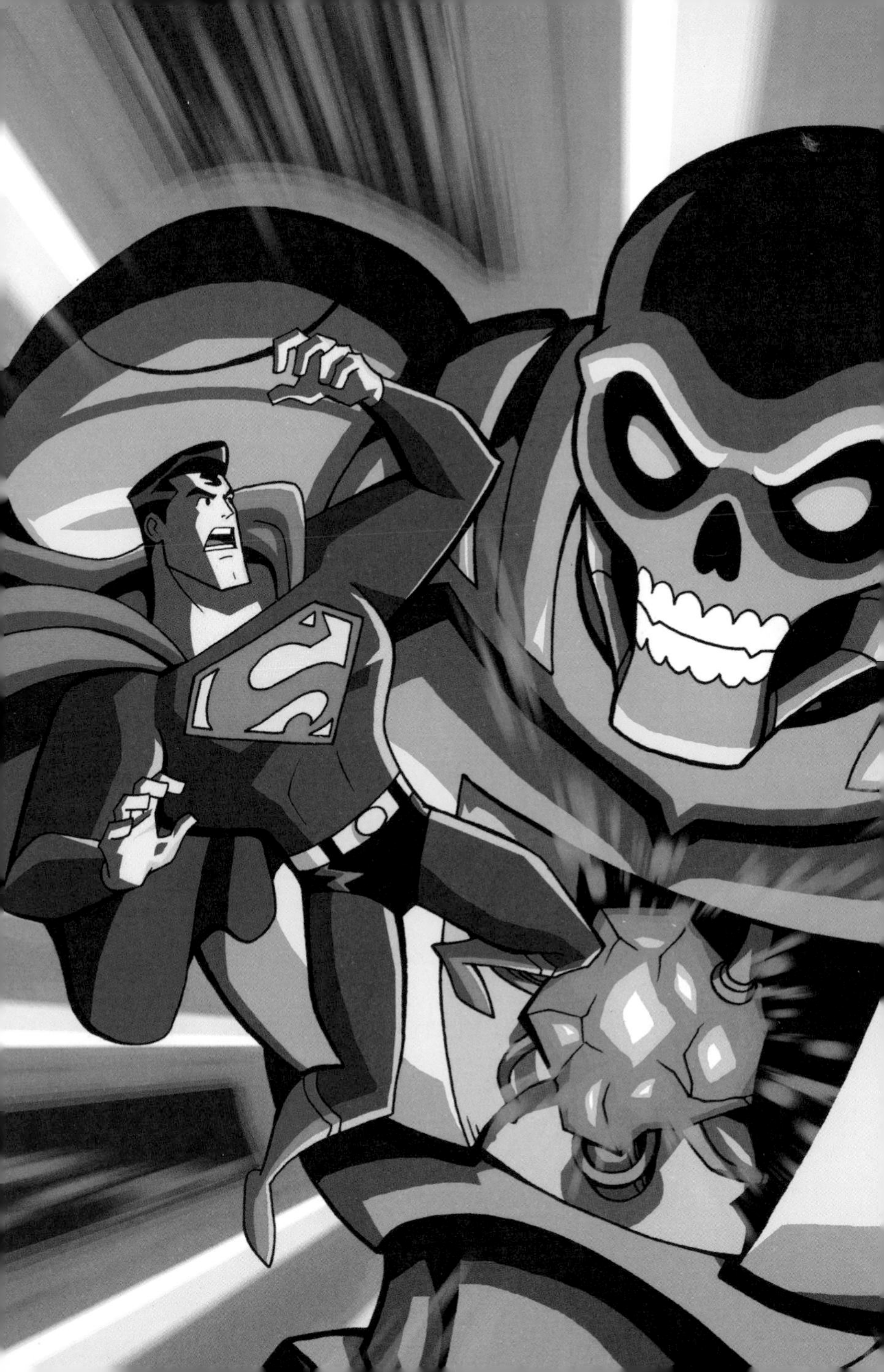

"Kryptonite!" Superman gasped. The hero immediately began to feel weak.

He tried to escape the Kryptonite's glow, but lost his balance. Dizzy, the Man of Steel fell and plummeted to the pavement.

THUD! Bizarro and the siblings arrived just after Superman crash-landed onto the street. Metallo lifted his giant foot, then brought it down hard on the weakened Man of Steel. **STOMP!**

"Listen to me, Bizarro," Marc said. "That green rock is hurting Superman. You need to destroy it!"

"Green rock bad," Bizarro said, nodding.

SLAM! Bizarro barreled head first into Metallo, sending the robot careening into a row of parked cars. The screeching sound of scraping metal was ear-piercing.

"Another Superman?" Metallo shouted.

"Me no Superman!" Bizarro shouted back. "Me am BIZARRO!"

"It doesn't matter," Metallo said. "I will destroy you just the same!"

Metallo lifted himself up. He charged at Bizarro, exposing the Kryptonite heart in his core. However, the stone's radiation had no effect on the duplicate.

"How is this possible?" Metallo cried.

"Green rock bad!" Bizarro said again. He took a deep breath and belched a fiery projectile square into Metallo's chest. **KIRRRRRRRRSH!** The blast of flames melted the meteorite until nothing was left.

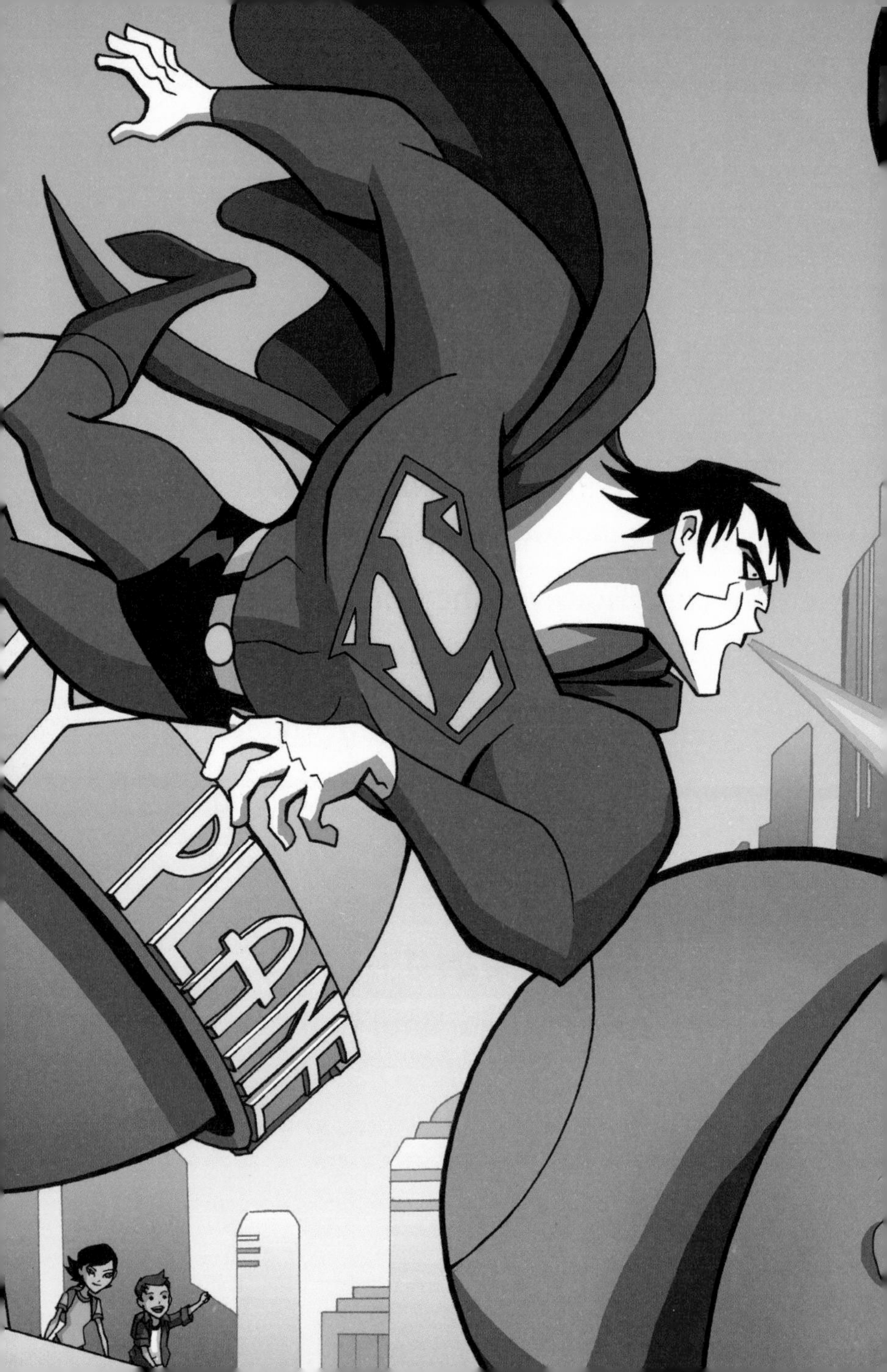
PLANE

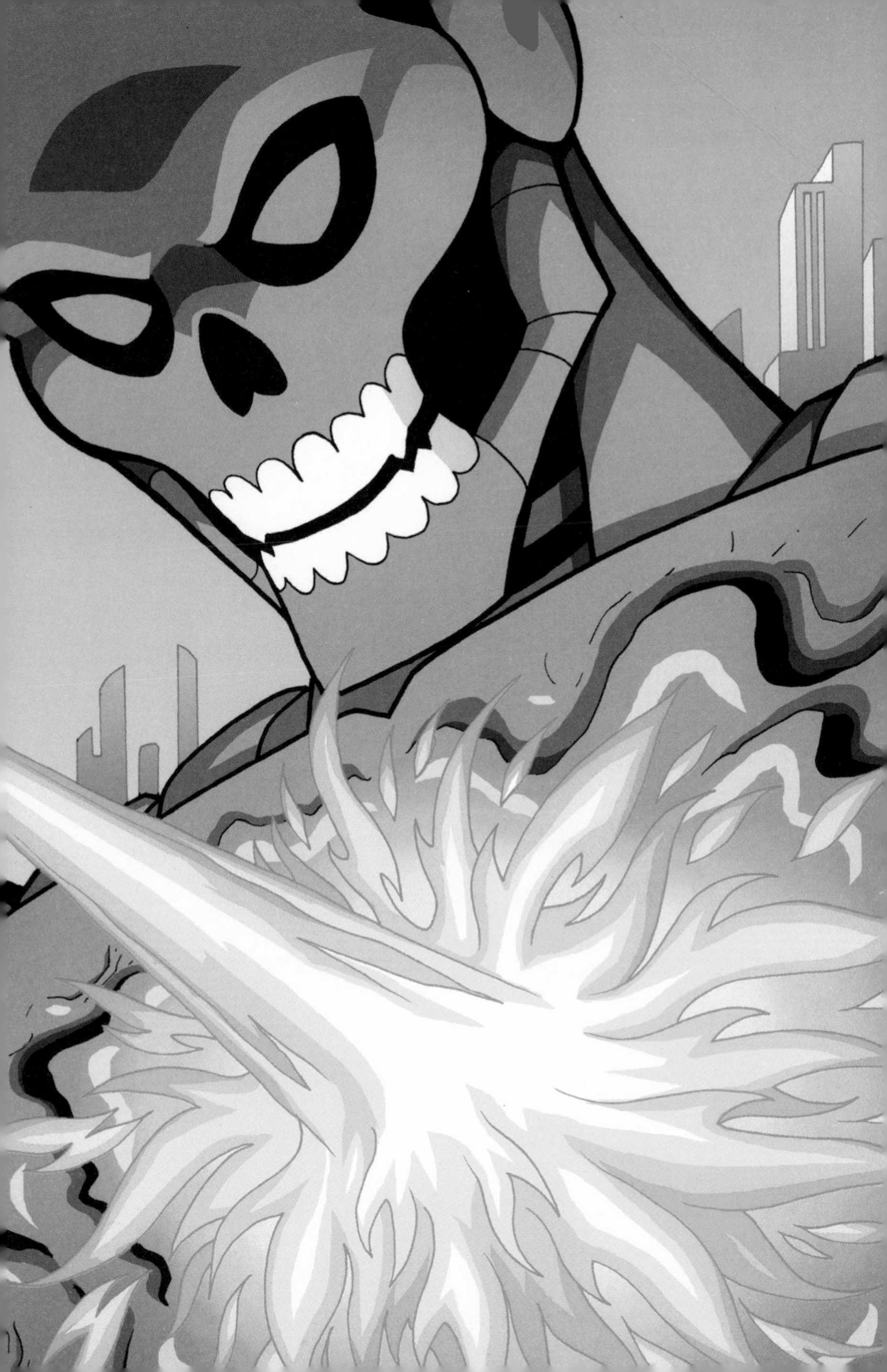

CHAPTER 5

BIZARRO THE HERO

With the deadly threat eliminated, Superman slowly regained his strength and abilities. Bizarro flew down to help the hero get back on his feet.

"Bizarro?" Superman said faintly. "But how did you escape?"

Metallo roared and snatched the distracted doppelganger in his fist. He squeezed tighter and tighter, hoping to crush his new nemesis, but Bizarro was invulnerable — just like the Man of Steel.

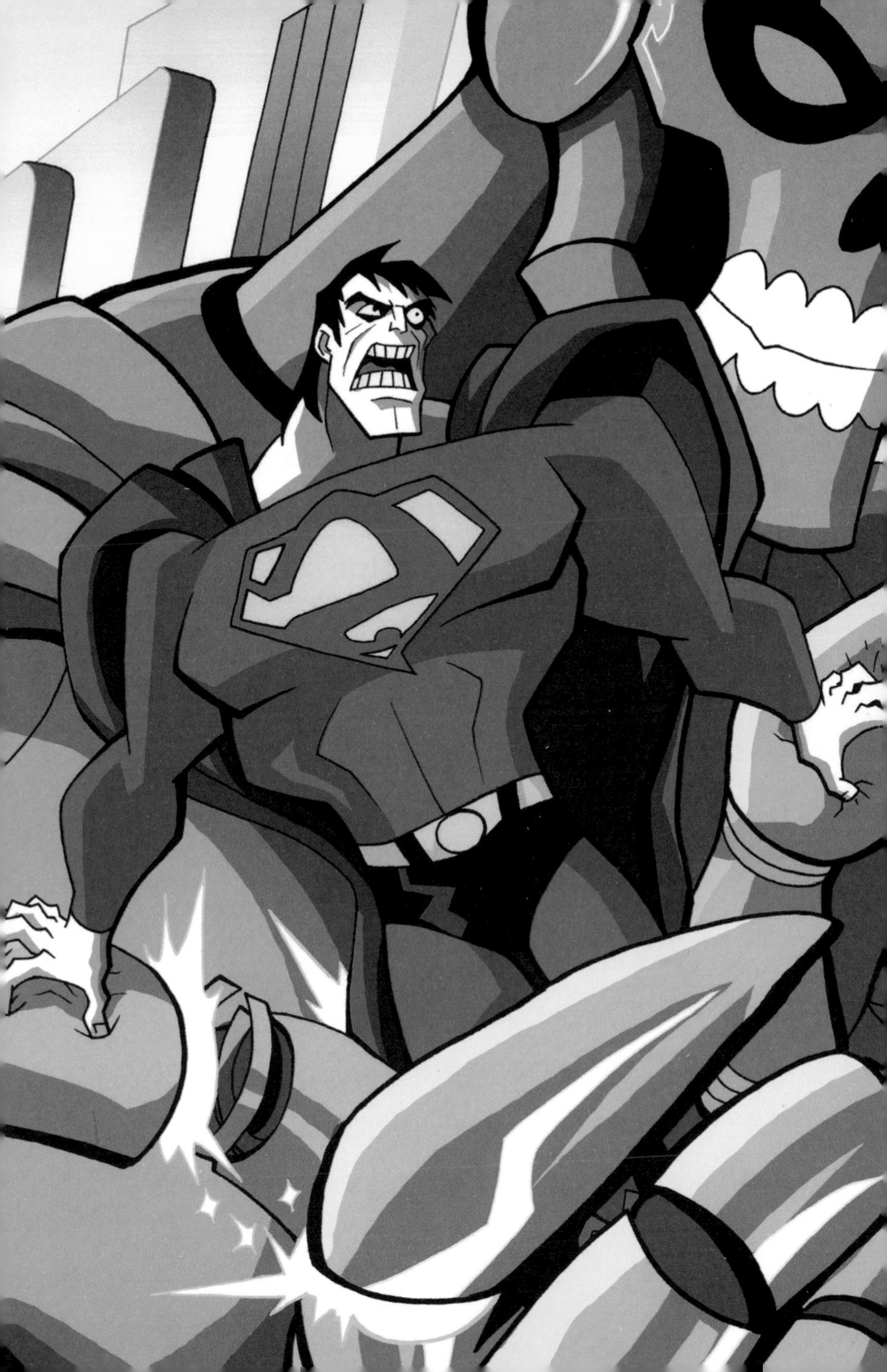

Bizarro lashed his arms out, breaking two of Metallo's fingers. **CRUNCH!** The giant robot was forced to release his grip.

"This is fun!" Bizarro said. "Me give metal man a hand!"

Bizarro grabbed Metallo's arm with both hands and heaved with all his might. **CRACK!** It ripped from the socket. Sparking wires stuck out from the robot's shoulder.

Bizarro carelessly hurled the limb over his shoulder. **WOOOSH!**

The discarded debris sailed through the air, heading straight for Anna and Marc! The youngsters were frozen with fear.

Luckily, Superman was quick enough to use his heat vision. He unleashed two red beams of blazing hot energy from his eyes with laser accuracy.

ZAP! ZRRRRRT!

The gloopy remains splashed onto the ground a hundred feet short of the siblings.

Marc cheered. "We have to take cover!" he said. The siblings found a safe spot inside the Daily Planet Building's lobby.

Bizarro spoke to Superman. "Me am here to help!" he said proudly.

"Fine," Superman said sternly. "But after, you and I are going to have a talk."

Suddenly, Metallo's foot came stomping down between the two caped comrades.

KABOOOOM!

It sent them flying to opposite sides of the street. "I'll destroy you both!" Metallo roared.

Bizarro recovered first.

Bizarro flew up to Metallo's chin.
He wound up and delivered a powerful
uppercut.

KAPOW!

The massive blow caused Metallo to reel
backward — straight into an uppercut from
Superman!

KA-BLAM!

Bizarro and Superman delivered a
flurry of punches that sent Metallo back
and forth between them like the ball in a
superpowered game of Ping-Pong.

Finally, the cyborg malfunctioned.

ZRRRT! ZRRRT! It dropped to its
knees.

"Bizarro, give Metallo an eyeful!"
Superman ordered.

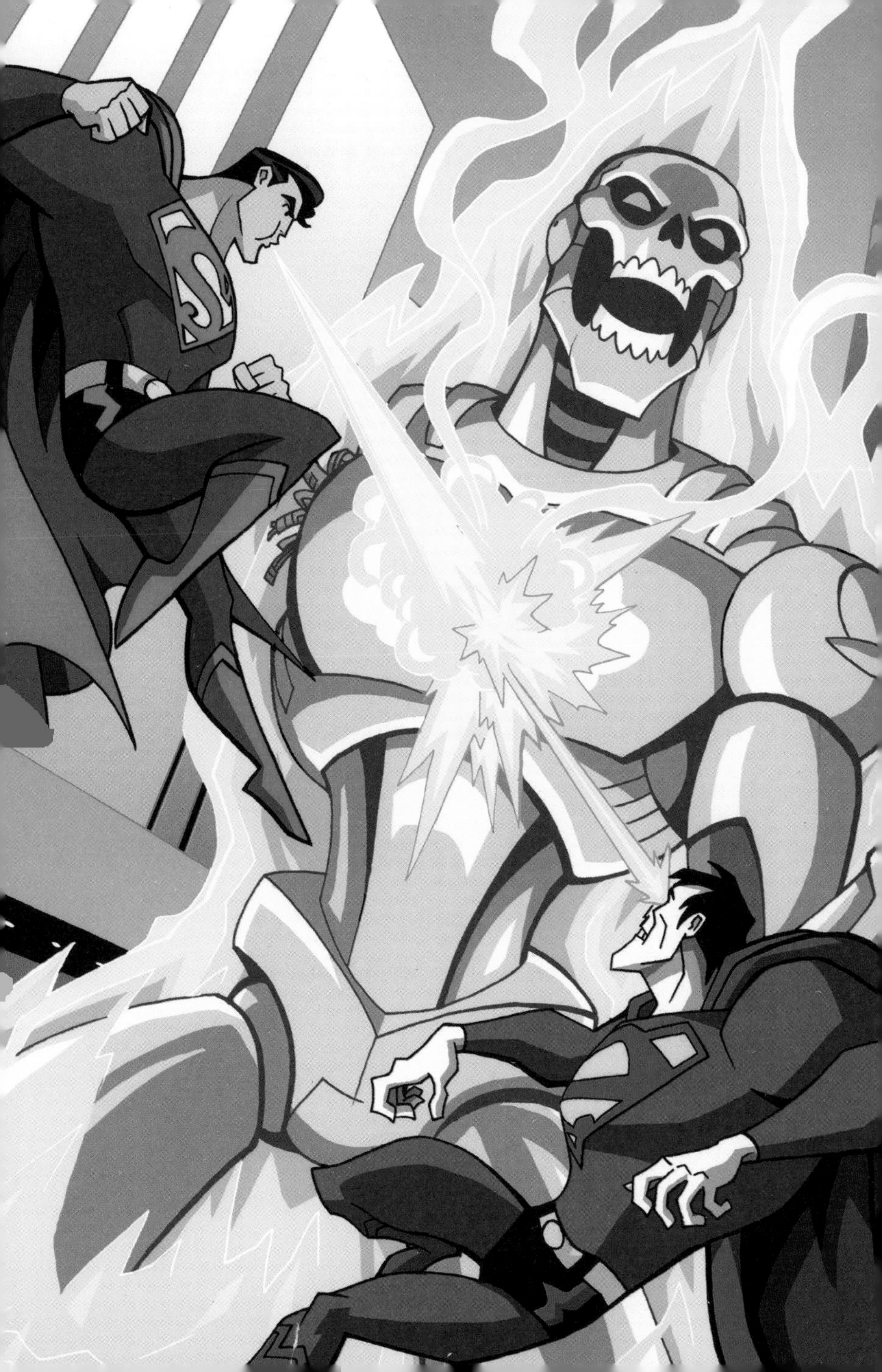

Bizarro aimed his freeze vision at the robotic menace.

CRACKLE!

Superman used his freeze breath simultaneously.

KIRRRRSH!

The arctic assault shut down Metallo's brain. The super-villain could no longer control his robot parts. Now completely encased in ice, Metallo was nothing more than a statue in front of the Daily Planet Building.

Lois Lane and Jimmy Olsen exited the building with their reporter gear ready to survey the scene.

"Wow!" Jimmy exclaimed. "I'm seeing double!" The young photographer snapped photos of Superman and Bizarro.

The Man of Steel turned to Bizarro with a furrowed brow. "So, Bizarro," he said. "How did you escape?"

"I can answer that," Lois replied with her cell phone in hand. "I got Dr. Hamilton from S.T.A.R. Labs on the phone a few minutes ago. He explained everything. There was a mishap at the facility, and Bizarro's stasis was interrupted. He was able to escape from his pod. Dr. Hamilton is extremely sorry and accepts all responsibility."

Superman frowned as he turned to face Bizarro. "I'm worried that you're still dangerous, Bizarro," he said. "You put those youngsters in harm's way when you carelessly threw Metallo's arm."

Bizarro hung his head. Marc and Anna came out of hiding.

The two kids stood by their new friend.

"Bizarro just wanted to be a hero," Marc said to Superman.

"He wanted us to write stories and take pictures like Lois and Jimmy do for you," added Anna.

Superman's features softened. "Bizarro, you are a hero," he admitted. "Without your help, the damage caused by Metallo would have been much more devastating. You saved Metropolis and you saved me. Thank you."

Bizarro's eyes widened. "Me am hero?" he asked.

"Well, we need to work on your situational awareness," Superman said, chuckling, "but yes. You have the heart of a hero."

Superman held out his hand. Bizarro shook it.

"Me am hero!" Bizarro cheered. He danced around Marc and Anna. "Bizarro am hero because Bizarro has three best friends!"

SUPER HEROES VS.

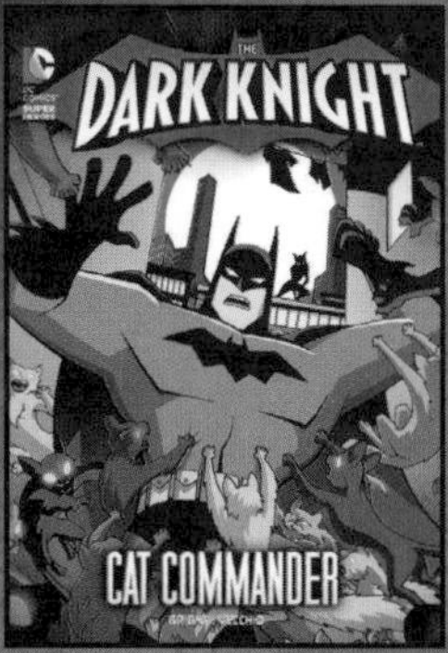
THE DARK KNIGHT
CAT COMMANDER
THE DARK KNIGHT: CAT COMMANDER

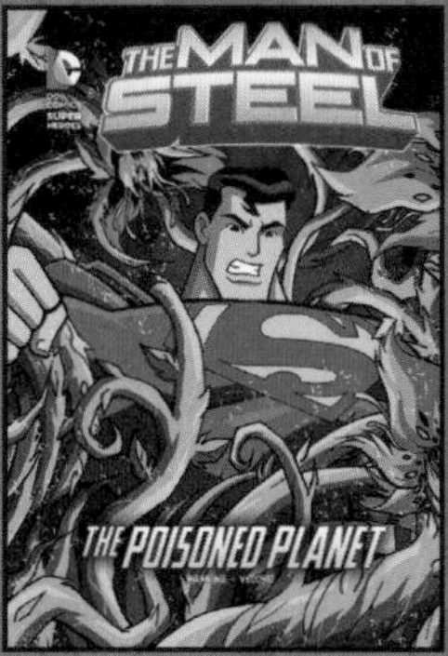
THE MAN OF STEEL
THE POISONED PLANET
THE MAN OF STEEL: THE POISONED PLANET

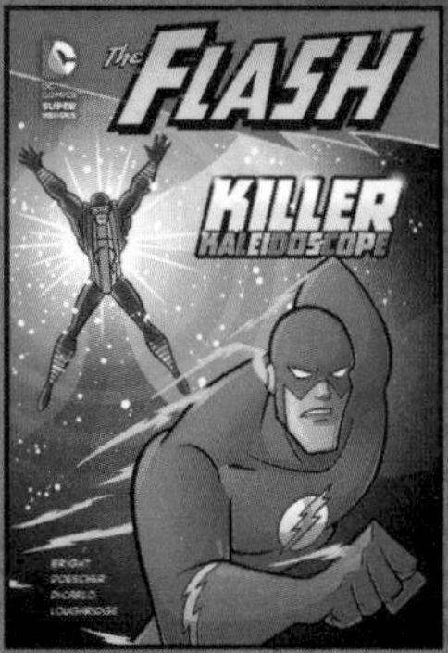
The FLASH
KILLER KALEIDOSCOPE
THE FLASH: KILLER KALEIDOSCOPE

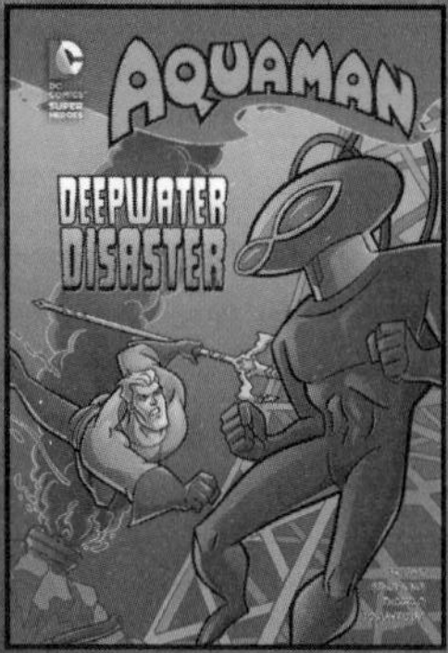
AQUAMAN
DEEPWATER DISASTER
AQUAMAN: DEEPWATER DISASTER

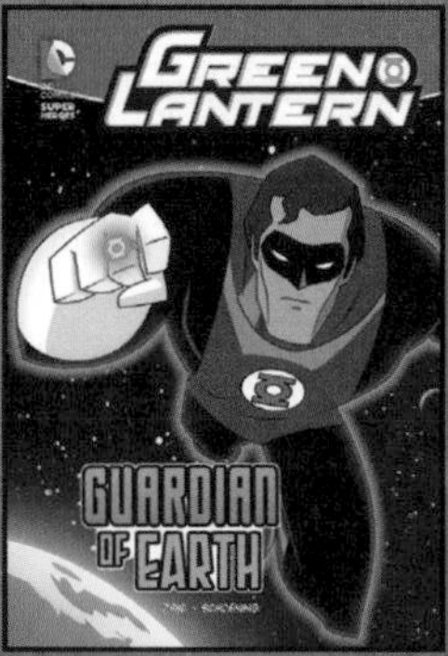
GREEN LANTERN
GUARDIAN OF EARTH
GREEN LANTERN: GUARDIAN OF EARTH

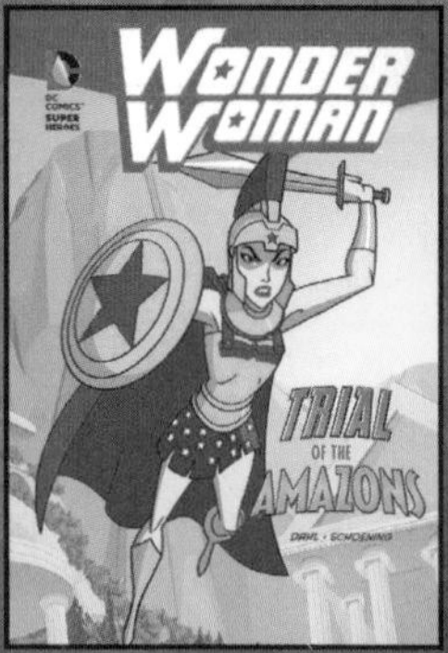
WONDER WOMAN
TRIAL OF THE AMAZONS
WONDER WOMAN: TRIAL OF THE AMAZONS

WHICH SIDE...

SUPER-VILLAINS

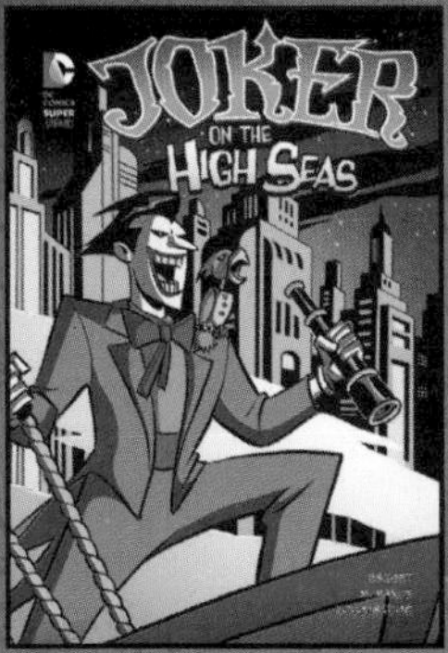
JOKER
ON THE
HIGH SEAS

JOKER ON THE HIGH SEAS

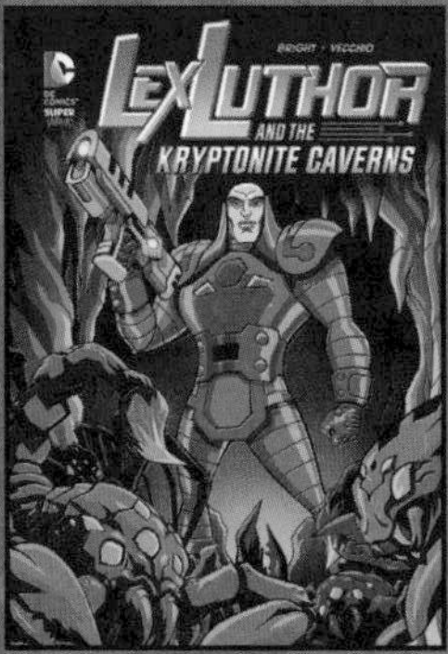
LEX LUTHOR
AND THE
KRYPTONITE CAVERNS

LEX LUTHOR AND THE KRYPTONITE CAVERNS

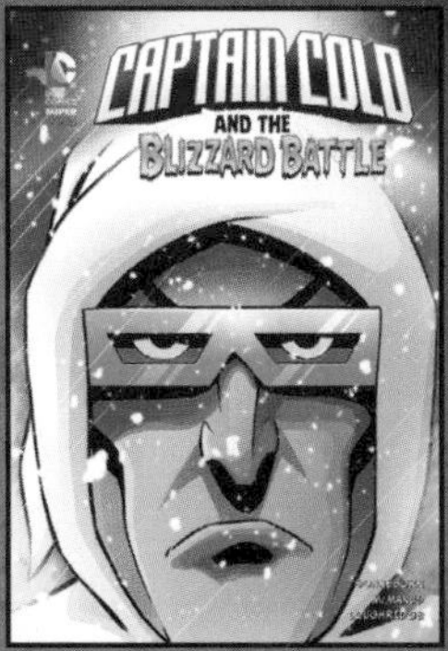
CAPTAIN COLD
AND THE
BLIZZARD BATTLE

CAPTAIN COLD AND THE BLIZZARD BATTLE

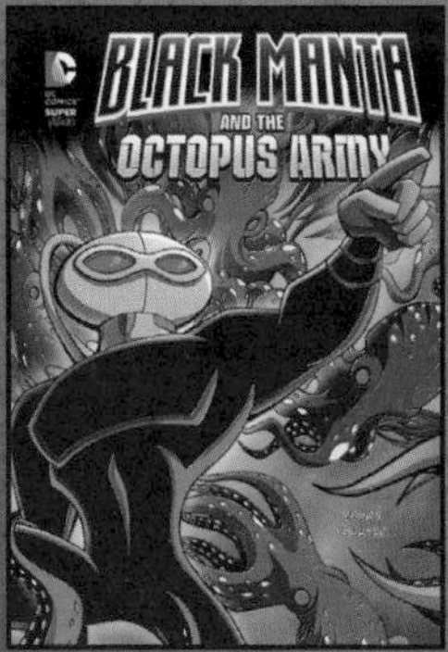
BLACK MANTA
AND THE
OCTOPUS ARMY

BLACK MANTA AND THE OCTOPUS ARMY

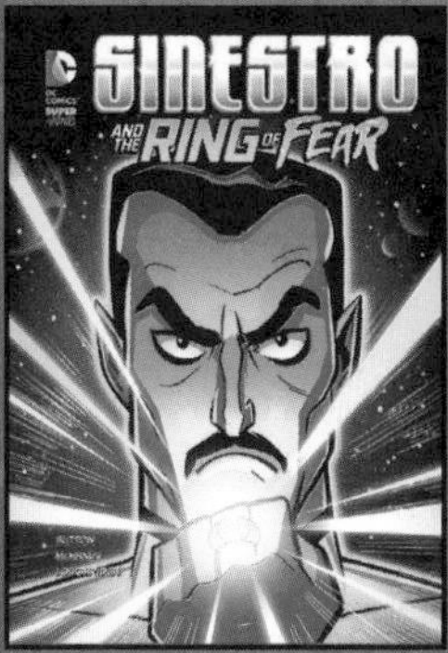
SINESTRO
AND THE RING OF FEAR

SINESTRO AND THE RING OF FEAR

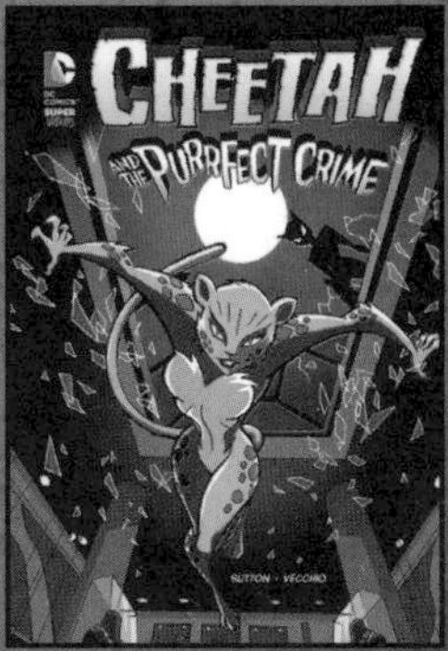
CHEETAH
AND THE PURRFECT CRIME

CHEETAH AND THE PURRFECT CRIME

WILL YOU CHOOSE?

IF YOU WERE SUPERMAN

Superman has many superpowers.
Of all the superpowers used by
Superman and Bizarro in this
book, which one would you want
to have the most? Why?

Superman's one weakness is his
vulnerability to Kryptonite. What
weaknesses do you have?

IF YOU WERE BIZARRO

Bizarro tries his best to do the right thing, but usually messes things up more than he helps. What mistakes have you made? How will you prevent them from happening again?

Despite Bizarro's good intentions, he is dangerous. Pretend you're Marc or Anna--what would you say to Bizarro to help him understand why he's dangerous?

AUTHOR BIO

John Sazaklis spent part of life working in a family coffee shop, the House of Donuts. The other part, he spent drawing and writing stories. He has illustrated Spider-Man books and written Batman books for HarperCollins. He has also created toys used in MAD Magazine.

SUPER HERO GLOSSARY

Daily Planet—the *Daily Planet* is a newspaper where Superman's friends Lois Lane and Jimmy Olsen work

freeze breath (FREEZ BRETH)—Superman can emit frigid bursts of cold from his lungs

heat vision (HEET VIZH-uhn)—Superman can fire powerful solar rays from his eyes

Krypton (KRIP-tahn)—Superman's home planet

S.T.A.R. Labs —a top-secret science facility. Professor Hamilton, a scientist who works there, often helps Superman with technology.

X-ray vision (EKS-ray VIZH-uhn)—Superman can see through solid objects (except for lead)

ILLUSTRATOR BIO

Luciano Vecchio was born in 1982 and currently lives in Buenos Aires, Argentina. With experience in illustration, animation, and comics, his works have been published in the US, Spain, UK, France, and Argentina. His credits include Ben 10 (DC Comics), Cruel Thing (Norma), Unseen Tribe (Zuda Comics), and Sentinels (Drumfish Productions).

SUPER-VILLAIN GLOSSARY

cryogenics (kry-oh-JEN-iks)—a field of science dealing with very low temperatures. Bizarro was put in cryostasis, or frozen, to keep him under control.

doppelganger (DOP-uhl-gang-ur)—a ghastly copy or double. Bizarro is Superman's doppelganger.

fire breath (FYE-ur BRETH)—while Superman can emit intense bursts of cold from his lungs, Bizarro can spit forth ultra-hot gouts of flame

freeze vision (FREEZ VIZH-uhn)—whereas Superman can fire solar energy from his eyes, Bizarro can fire bursts of intense cold

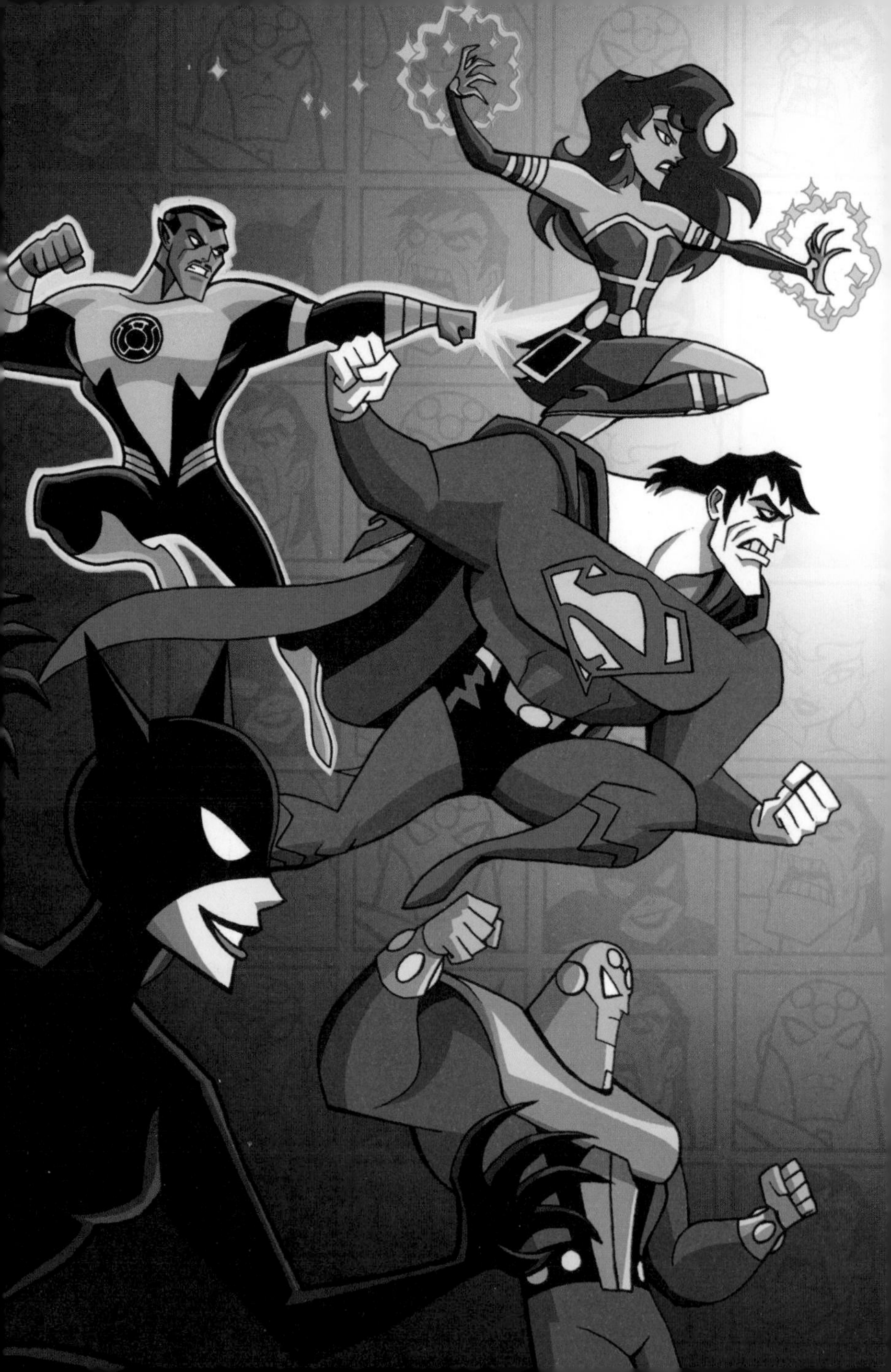